D0005410

Goldilocks and the Three Bears

First published in 2012 by
The Puppet Company Ltd
Units 2–4 Cam Centre
Wilbury Way
Hitchin
Herts
SG4 0TW

www.thepuppetcompany.com

Text copyright © Sue Lockey, 2012
Illustrations copyright © Sandra Evans, 2012

All rights reserved. No part of this publication may be
reproduced, stored or transmitted in any form without
the express written permission of the publisher

ISBN: 978-1-908633-01-9

British Library Cataloguing-in-Publication Data
A catalogue record for this book is available
from the British Library

Printed in China

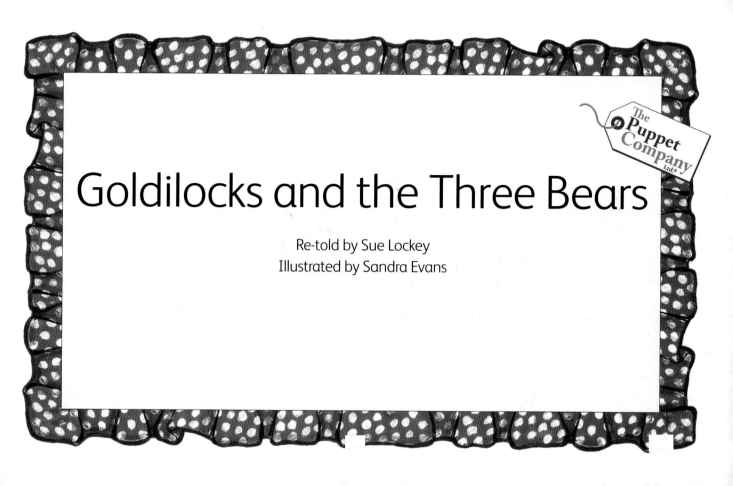

Goldilocks and the Three Bears

Re-told by Sue Lockey
Illustrated by Sandra Evans

The Puppet Company Ltd®

Once upon a time there was a little girl called Goldilocks who lived with her mother in a little house at the edge of the woods.

One morning, Goldilocks decided to go into the woods to pick some beautiful flowers for her mother.

She forgot that her mother had told her never to go into the woods on her own.

Soon she was lost, but she saw a little cottage that belonged to three bears who had gone out for a walk.

Goldilocks went into the cottage without being invited.

On the table were three bowls of porridge – a large bowl for Daddy Bear, a medium-sized bowl for Mummy Bear, and a small bowl for Baby Bear.

Goldilocks was so hungry that she forgot her manners! She took a spoonful of porridge from the largest bowl.

"Oh, this is much too hot for me," she said, and she moved to the medium-sized bowl.

"Oh, this is much too lumpy for me," she said, and she moved to the small bowl.

"Oh, this is just right for me," said Goldilocks, and she ate it all up!

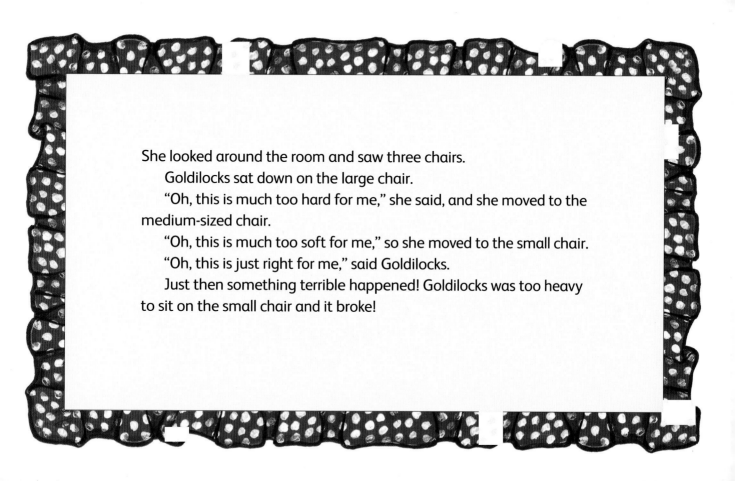

She looked around the room and saw three chairs.

Goldilocks sat down on the large chair.

"Oh, this is much too hard for me," she said, and she moved to the medium-sized chair.

"Oh, this is much too soft for me," so she moved to the small chair.

"Oh, this is just right for me," said Goldilocks.

Just then something terrible happened! Goldilocks was too heavy to sit on the small chair and it broke!

Goldilocks rushed upstairs and found three beds in the bedroom. She was feeling very tired and lay down on the large bed.

"Oh, this is too hard and uncomfortable for me," said Goldilocks, and she moved to the medium-sized bed.

"Oh, this is too soft and lumpy for me," said Goldilocks, and she moved to the smallest bed.

"Oh, this is just right for me," said Goldilocks, and soon she was fast asleep.

By now, the bears had finished their walk in the woods and were hungry and ready for their breakfast.

"Who has been eating my porridge?" roared Daddy Bear when he saw that some of his breakfast had been eaten.

"Who has been eating my porridge?" exclaimed Mummy Bear when she saw that some of her breakfast had been eaten.

"Who has been eating my porridge – and has eaten it all up?" wailed Baby Bear. The three bears were not very happy!

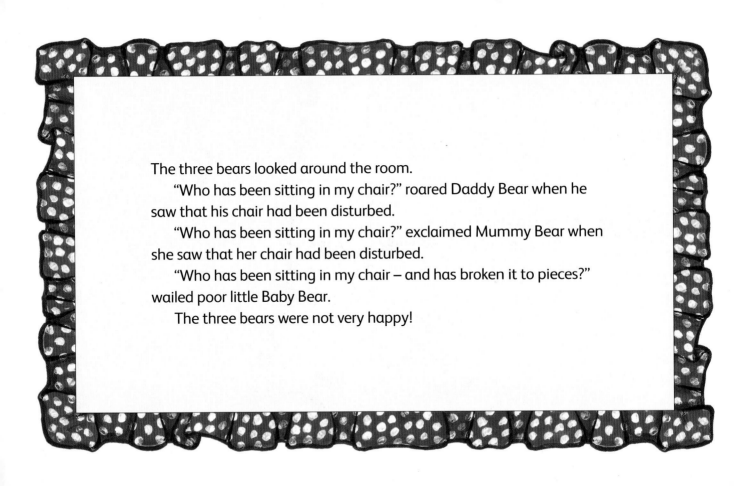

The three bears looked around the room.

"Who has been sitting in my chair?" roared Daddy Bear when he saw that his chair had been disturbed.

"Who has been sitting in my chair?" exclaimed Mummy Bear when she saw that her chair had been disturbed.

"Who has been sitting in my chair – and has broken it to pieces?" wailed poor little Baby Bear.

The three bears were not very happy!

The three bears went upstairs to their bedroom.

"Who has been sleeping in my bed?" roared Daddy Bear when he saw that his bed had been slept in.

"Who has been sleeping in my bed?" exclaimed Mummy Bear when she saw that her bed had been slept in.

"Who has been sleeping in my bed – and look, she's still there!" wailed poor little Baby Bear.

The three bears were not very happy!

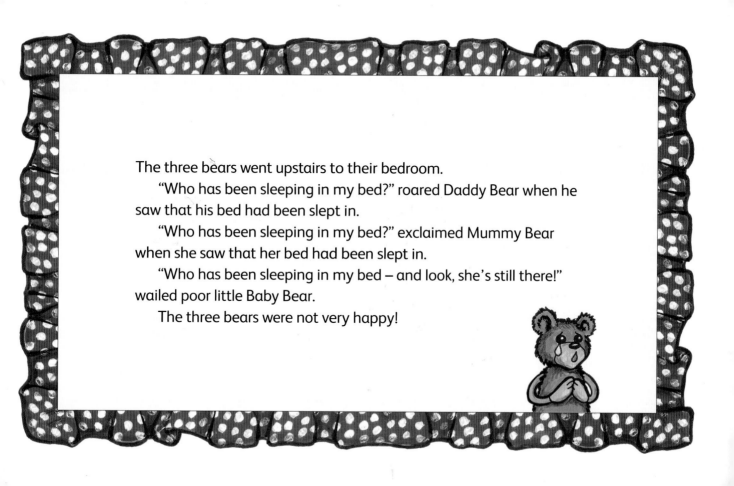

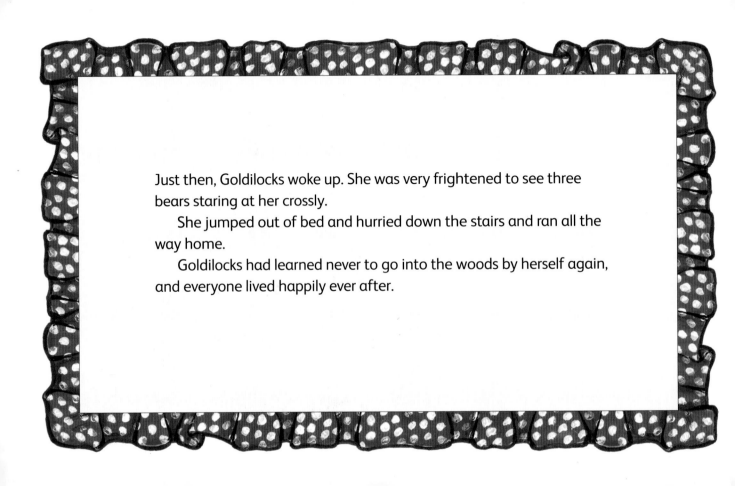

Just then, Goldilocks woke up. She was very frightened to see three bears staring at her crossly.

She jumped out of bed and hurried down the stairs and ran all the way home.

Goldilocks had learned never to go into the woods by herself again, and everyone lived happily ever after.

Two pictures for you to colour in.